THE LETTERS PAGE

Vol. 2

©2017 BOOK EX MACHINA, Nicosia, Cyprus

Mailing address: P.O. Box 23595, Nicosia 1685, Cyprus. We love mail (yeah we do!), and we'd love it if you write to us. (To send letters to *The Letters Page* please use their address below.) Our website is bookexmachina.com

Book & cover design: Ioanna Mavrou & Thodoris Tzalavras

Illustrations: Thodoris Tzalavras

Printed in Malaysia

The Letters Page, a literary journal in letters, is a project run within the creative writing section of the School of English at the University of Nottingham, and is entirely funded by the University of Nottingham. Details of both undergraduate and postgraduate courses can be found at nottingham.ac.uk/english

These are the excellent people who make the whole thing possible:

Editor: Jon McGregor; office manager: Annalise Grice and Leah Wilkins; administrative support: Rebecca Peck, Mari Hughes, Emma Zimmerman; technical support: Stephen McKibbin, Ed Downey; copy-editing: Gillian Roberts; editorial assistance: Rachael Smart.

Editorial Board: Naomi Alderman, Tash Aw, Roddy Doyle, Patricia Duncker, William Fiennes, Chris Gribble, Sarah Hall, Kirsten Harris, Chloe Hooper, Mick Jackson, Benjamin Johncock, Cormac Kinsella, Katie Kitamura, Éireann Lorsung, Colum McCann, Maile Meloy, Kei Miller, Nick Mount, Emily Perkins, Julie Sanders, Kamila Shamsie, Nikesh Shukla, Craig Taylor, Xu Xi.

The Letters Page can be found at www.theletterspage.ac.uk and you can submit your letters to: *The Letters Page*, School of English, University of Nottingham, NG7 2RD, U.K.

This is volume 2 in our *The Letters Page* series. Last year, in 2016, we published *The Letters Page, Vol. 1*, a beautiful limited-edition boxed set.

THE LETTERS PAGE
Vol. 2

Edited by Jon McGregor

BOOK EX MACHINA
NICOSIA

CONTENTS

IOANNA MAVROU
A Letter from the Publisher 9

JOE DUNTHORNE
Delete These Excess Letters 15

KIT CALESS
Who Knows the Origin of Anything? 21

NICOLE FLATTERY
It Felt Like a Secret 29

ANDREW McMILLAN
We're All Plagiarists of Each Other 35

CHIMENE SULEYMAN
Tables Forty Years Untouched 39

DARREN CHETTY
Thou Shalt Not Steal 43

ROWENA MACDONALD
They Don't Know Why He's Worried About Copyright 49

SARAH DALE
No-One Leaves This Town Dehydrated 55

JONATHAN ELLIS
I'm Not Sure Who This Is Addressed to 59

MATTHEW WELTON
Five Pieces of 250 Words: A Bibliography 65

JON McGREGOR
A Letter from the Editor 75

Copies are everything

Ioanna Mavrou
Nicosia, Cyprus

Dear Reader,

Hello. I hope that this letter finds you well, wherever you are. Thank you for picking up this book. It's nice, isn't it, to pick up a book and sit with it for a while, letting the rest of the world go by, as if stepping out of the world for a beat and taking a much needed breath—this is how it feels to me anyway, sitting here writing you this letter. I sit here, outside the world for a beat, writing a letter to a complete stranger, and you could be anyone, and I could be anyone, but as this is a letter from the publisher[1] even though we are strangers we already have something in common and a relationship, sort of: you, a reader of books, and me, a publisher of.

By the time you read this it will be early fall and we, the publishers, will be eagerly awaiting word re: your thoughts on this new volume, our second one in *The Letters Page* series. Are you enjoying it? Is the typesetting and design and paper aesthetically pleasing? Do you love these letters as much as we do? Are you going to tell your friends, family, and strangers on the internet about it? Will you be inspired to write us or the editor, Jon McGregor, lovely letters, perhaps for a future volume?[2]

But, as I sit here writing to you, we are not really thinking about any of these things yet. Right now it's still March and time just sprang forward, and the fig tree outside the house just sprouted new leaves and we are thinking a lot about copies, which is the theme of this volume that you are now reading/are about to read.

I've been thinking a lot about the concept of copies even before Jon picked it as a theme for this volume. There's the whole issue of copyrights that every writer and publisher considers at some point in their lives/careers/work. (Some more on that later.[3]) And I've been thinking about copies and books:

A copy of a book arrives in the mail in a neat little envelope with buttons and a string. Inside, there are copies of letters, transcripts of letters typeset in an aesthetically pleasing and readable typeface. (No offense to the letter-writers; my own handwriting is barely legible.) One of these copies is what you now hold in your hands. Almost everything written comes to us via the act of making copies. Thousands of years ago a text would arrive at the hands of its readers[4] on a clay tablet. *The Epic of Gilgamesh*, say, or a story of a great flood and an ark,[5] or a recipe for date pistachio balls.[6] Then, later, text appeared on scrolls, then in handwritten, hand-copied, and hand-sewn books, and finally in typeset printed books such as this one, more or less. (And e-books. It took thousands of years of writing and printing technology to get here, and now we have electronic copies of texts.[7])

I've also been thinking about copies and music: We tend to take the current paradigm (music industry, current technologies, etc.) as the way of things but, just like words, music has been reaching its listeners in lots of different ways since prehistoric times in copies: from versions of the original in multiple performances of the same piece, to gramophone records, to records, to cassette tapes, to CDs, to digital files (MP3s, lossless audio, etc.)

And it's not just books or music. Almost all[8] of our human knowledge and thoughts and beliefs, science and observations, and versions of history have survived, been transmitted, and evolved via copies. Copies are everything. Human life itself is copies. Without copies there's no life, literally. There's just one lonely cell in the primordial waters not dividing, not copying itself to evolution and posterity but just dying out all by its lonesome singleness and then life as we know it on planet Earth never happens—but because copies are everywhere life exists. Copies are in your cells, in your DNA, and in those of our ancestors and descendants, copying repeatedly, making life possible; this is how life began and how it evolved and how it continues.

So basically, yay, copies! Think about that next time you pass by a library, or hear about a seed bank, or listen to a song playing on your preferred medium. Speaking of songs, here's a little observation about the whole copyright legal debate that's been stuck in my head for a while. It's that old and much universally mocked warning that used to autoplay in the beginning of DVDs (remember those? I don't even have a player anymore, I just look at them, all those store-bought copies of movies and TV shows, gathering dust on my shelves …) "Would you steal a car?" Would *you* steal a car? No. Would you *download* a car? Yes, I would download a car! Hell yes. A thousand times yes. If you knew the car was safe and would drive well and no one would miss it because it was just a copy of a car that also existed elsewhere, the original car unaffected by the download, both existing simultaneously … it's as Kit Caless says, in his letter, "analogue analogies just don't seem to work." You think of copies as physical things, *would you steal a car?*, but it's not where we are anymore, and who knows where we're headed.

Anyway, as with most letters, I'm rumbling on and it's getting late. I have this book to publish and you have this book to read. I hope you enjoy it and thanks again for picking it up and spending time with it, precious time that you could spend reading something else, or walking outside on this lovely fall day.[9] I hope you have a good one.

My best wishes,

The publisher

P.S. Here's a little short story I wrote re: copies.

You can't stand the world so you make a copy of it and look at it instead. There's a copy of everything, there's even a copy-Twitter where people speak of things that happen in the copy world. The two worlds are not identical, they are parallel universes. Maybe if you make enough copies of worlds, a copy of a copy of a copy enough times, maybe you'll make it all the way home.

---

1 Actually, there are two of us: for more info see bookexmachina.com/about.html

2 We hope so; our mailing addresses (and that of *The Letters Page*) are on the cover, the copyright page, and on the envelope.

3 If you're interested in copyright issues, I would refer you to anything written by Cory Doctorow on the matter: craphound.com/tag/copyfight/ ; also check out EFF (Electronic Freedom Foundation): eff.org/

4 Although at that time readers as well as writers were very few, with writing being this new technology mostly used by the elite. And, for example cuneiform is a little more difficult than say, English.

5 For more see: theguardian.com/books/2014/feb/11/noahs-ark-round-ancient-british-museum-mesopotamian-clay-tablets-flood This is an indication that human knowledge, experience, and ideas repeat themselves: copies and versions appearing over and over again.

6 As per a Mesopotamian tablet found in Mari: *1 cup dates, 1 cup pistachios.* (The rest is up to the reader's imagination. Also there's some debate about whether the second word means pistachios or terebinths. After trying it, we can confirm that the interpretation of this recipe, with either pistachios or terebinths, found on globaltableadventure.com/recipe/pistachio-date-balls/ works great.)

7 As a publisher of printed books I am obligated to tell you that current research and sales figures show most people (young people, too) still prefer print books to e-books.

8 Yes, oral traditions, which are just as important, are copies too, oral copies transmitted and repeated again and again through generations.

9 Seriously, will you write and tell us how it is where you are? Our addresses are included etc., etc.

delcte

these

excess

letters

Joe Dunthorne
Swansea

Sweetness, Sweetness,

The cells smell fresh. The bedsheets feel new. The gentle breeze wends between the beeches, the yews, the elms; the slender trees lend the ten-metre fence serene resplendence. We never feel repressed, never resent the screws' keys.

Remember, Sweetness, when we revered "free speech"—"free speech," we yelled! "We, the rebels, reject depleted texts!" We sneered whenever we met well-dressed gentlemen yet, Sweetness, *we* were the sheep. We were the pretenders. The well-dressed gentlemen: they knew best.

The well-dressed gentlemen helped me see: the less speech the better.

The well-dressed gentlemen helped me delete these excess letters.

The pens the gentlemen lent me spell the letter e best, hence the preference.

Sweetness, we never needed every verb, every sentence. The letter e, yes, yet let the rest rest. Let the stress end.

The screws here keep me well fed; we need never feel tense.

Elevenses, they serve sweet crêpes.

Three p.m., they send the Greek meze: cheese, eggs, herb-scented bell peppers.

Seven p.m., they serve beef cheeks en crème, shelled whelks, fresh greens, stewed fennel, Welsh leeks, French cheeses, bejewelled desserts. Crème de menthe helps the feed settle.

Eleven p.m., the bell knells then we enter deep sleep.

See, Sweetness, these cells represent the new Eden. The well-dressed gentlemen's cleverness renders me speechless.

Hence, we let the clever well-dressed gentlemen see where we keep the secret den.

Hence, when the well-dressed men descend, let them enter, Sweetness, tell them: "yes yes yes."

Let them see the rebel texts. Let the texts be shredded.

Remember, Sweetness, the new Eden needs settlers. When we get wedded here, get preggers here, brew red beer, sell the kegs, breed red hens, sell the eggs: endless glee. Three cells between three: the three-bed des res, better rent terms, well-deserved rest.

Sweetness, Sweetness, be clever. Let the well-dressed gentlemen see we respect them.

Best,

Peter[1] x x x

P.S. They helped me select "Peter," the clever, clever men.[2]

1 This letter is not, in fact, from "Peter," but was written by Joe Dunthorne. Joe is a Welsh novelist, poet and journalist. He is a graduate of the University of East Anglia's creative writing MA, where he was awarded the Curtis Brown prize. His poetry has been published in magazines and anthologies and was featured on Channel 4, and BBC Radio 3 and 4. A pamphlet collection, *Joe Dunthorne: Faber New Poets 5*, was published in 2010.

Joe has published two novels: *Submarine*, which was made into a film, and *Wild Abandon*, which won the Society of Author's Encore award. His third novel, *The Adulterants*, will be published in early 2018. He recently completed the Trans-Siberian Lit, a travelling art residency with the British Council which is available to experience online at inrussia.com/storytellers

2 We asked Joe if he'd copied the idea for this letter from Georges Perec or the Oulipo group, and he said yes, in a manner of speaking, although he wouldn't call it "copying" as such. We asked him to expand, and he expanded thus:

"This letter is a univocalism, a piece of writing that only uses one vowel. One of the earliest univocalisms is a poem by C.C. Bombaugh from 1890 that contains this couplet:

No cool monsoons blow soft on Oxford dons,
Orthodox, jog-trot, book-worm Solomons!

I became interested in univocalic writing through the Oulipo, a group of writers and mathematicians, which formed in Paris in the Sixties. They use formal, often mathematical, structures as a way of composing literature.

The most famous member of the Oulipo is Georges Perec. He wrote a novella, *Les Revenentes*, that only uses the vowel "e." He also wrote a novel, *La Disparition*, that does not use the letter "e." *La Disparition* is a comic novel about absence. It is also, implicitly, about the Holocaust. Perec was born in 1936 to Polish Jews who'd emigrated to France in the twenties. His dad died from untreated shrapnel wounds sustained fighting for the French army in World War II and his mother was murded in Auschwitz. In 1942, aged sixteen, he was taken in by his aunt and uncle in France. When composing *La Disparition*, Perec could not write the words: père, mère, parents, famille, nor could he write his own name Georges Perec. *La Disparition* is a novel about disappearance, about the ease with which absences go unnoticed. The first reviews of the book didn't notice that he hadn't used the letter "e."

My letter was originally written for an Artangel project in Reading Prison. Twenty-two writers and artists were invited to create work that would be displayed inside one of the cells in the old Victorian jail. Among those cells was C.3.3., where Oscar Wilde spent nearly two years, having been convicted of gross indecency with other men. In 1895—when Wilde was there—the jail worked on the separate system: prisoners were kept in isolation and not allowed to speak with each other. Wilde had little access to books other than the Bible and was required to spend his day performing arbitrary manual tasks. After some time he was given literature and was enabled to write but only on one piece of paper at a time. He wrote a 50,000-word love/hate/regret letter to his former lover, Lord Alfred Douglas. The letter —now published as *De Profundis*—was kept in the prison and never sent. Wilde never recovered from his time in prison and died three years after his release. *De Profundis* was left unpublished until after his death.

In my letter, I imagine a jail in which restrictions are placed upon language itself. My prisoner is not allowed to use any vowel but "e." My prisoner, like Perec, cannot write his own name, so he is invited to become Peter. By constraining language, the jailers constrain the prisoner's ability to understand the world and to imagine other, better worlds."

who knows

the

origin of

anything?

(On Instagram Messenger)

Hi there,

I'm the guy who runs the Wetherspoon's Carpets Tumblr.[1] Just thought I'd send you a message to apologise for the post I wrote many months back. I could have just said "Hi" instead of calling you a prick. Anyway I just wanted to say, no hard feelings on the Instagram account you set up. I was a bit angry that you had copied the idea off me without saying hello or referencing the original. I know you started the Instagram account the day after the big piece in *The Guardian* about my blog because I can see the date the account was set up. You must have known about it.

I don't really mind. I think it's great that people are getting involved. I was more concerned that people might just send pictures to you, rather than me, and this would mean completing the blog would take much longer.

Anyhow, as I said, no hard feelings.

Best,

Kit

Hi again,

Thanks for the nice reply, and for offering to put a link for the bio for Tumblr. I will do the same, i.e. provide a link to your Insta on my Tumblr.[2] You seem to have gained a lot of followers since I last wrote, almost as many as me.

I don't believe that you didn't know about the Tumblr, but that's okay, it's the internet, who knows the origin of anything? Although, like I said, the timing of your Insta and mine going viral. But you know, I don't have intellectual property rights on compiling of other people's photos of carpets.[3] It's more that you literally copied what I was doing but on another format.

I keep trying to find comparisons for this like, "I made a film of your novel without telling you," but analogue analogies just don't seem to work. Not only do I admit I can't own the rights to compiling pictures of carpets, what does a different platform mean in terms of ownership? Why would I have ownership over the same idea on different platforms? On the other hand, why wouldn't I?

Regardless, glad we've come to an accord. If you'd like a pint sometime at Spoon's, gimme a shout, would be nice to meet a fellow enthusiast!

Best,

Kit

Hi once more,

I never considered you wouldn't live in London! How myopic of me. I've never been to [redacted] before, it seems nice. Glad to hear your kids are teaching you about Twitter. I'm amazed you know Instagram and not Twitter. I came to Insta much later because it's harder to have conversations and well, I'm a writer so Twitter is more my sort of medium.

You say your friend told you about the carpet thing so that means you didn't copy me. I'd like to think you could just admit you've been found out. But what's done is done. I've got no beef.

The copyright thing *is* murky.[4] Taking photos of carpet designs and logging it on a website isn't the world's greatest idea, I'll admit, and of course I didn't design the carpets in the first place so I suppose you're right, I am benefitting from someone else's creative work through my compilation of those designs. Moreover, I'm compiling other people's photos of other people's designs, so perhaps I don't have much of a leg to stand on. Even so, it's weird that you would want to copy this, considering those points you make disparage it. Or do you think that it invalidates your theft of my idea? Because I've stolen other people's work? I would say I was "celebrating the carpet designs." Does that mean you are celebrating my Tumblr, or celebrating the carpets entirely separately?

I'm doing a book soon, by the way. Which is cool.

Best,

Kit

Hi,

Thanks for the kind words about the book![5] I'm excited. I hope people like it. And thanks for the apology. You didn't have to say sorry, but I'm glad you did. I know it's such a small thing in the current climate, what with the world going to the dogs and everyone out for themselves, but it was kind of the principle of it that I felt I had to defend. You know the whole "fake news" thing? It felt like that really. Ultimately, I still don't understand where the joy is in it for you. I mean, do you genuinely like doing it knowing it's not your own idea and that people think you are me? It's weird but perhaps you really do.

I do appreciate you putting up a little note about the book too, it's kind. Though I noticed you deleted a day later. Perhaps by mistake? If you'd like to come to the book launch do let me know. Would be great to meet you in person, buy you a pint and put this behind us.

Take care,

Kit

Hello,

OK, no worries about the launch.

Thanks,

Kit

Hi,

Just to say, I think someone has sent you a false carpet picture to try and trick you into reposting something that isn't from the pub.

Hope all is well,

Kit

Hiya,

So the book is out now. Hope you don't have too many people asking you about it! If anyone, journalists or some such ask you for an interview by mistake just pass them to me, if you wouldn't mind? That would be great.

I'm really glad we sorted this out. Best of luck with your account, getting more followers and all that.

Kit[6]

---

1 wetherspoonscarpets.tumblr.com is a photographic record of the carpets found in branches of the U.K. pub chain Wetherspoon's. Each carpet is a unique design commissioned by the chain to complement the building's interior. When the Tumblr and Instagram accounts which the writer had set up were featured in *The Guardian*, a number of copycat Instagram accounts were set up in response. These letters were written to the founder of one of those.

2 "Insta" is used here as an abbreviation of Instagram, a popular photographic social network. "Tumblr" is the full name of the blogging platform Tumblr.

3 Intellectual property rights experts may disagree on this point. An analogy might be that of a poetry anthology, wherein the copyright of each poem would be held by the poet (or estate), but the anthologist would have copyright in the selection, sequencing, and arrangement of those poems. (Full disclosure: the editor is not a legal expert, and this footnote does not constitute legal advice, and it is definitely not ironic that this observation on intellectual property rights was cribbed from other people's work on the internet.)

4 It's not really. See previous footnote.

5 *Spoon's Carpets: An Appreciation*, by Kit Caless (Square Peg, 2016)

6 Kit Caless is a writer and broadcaster based in London. He is a regular contributor to *Vice Magazine* and to publications as varied as *Architectural Digest*, *The Quietus*, and *Ambit*. He has described himself as the "Shagpile Socrates." He is co-founder and editor at Influx Press, a small independent publisher of fiction and creative non-fiction. He lives in Hackney, London, which is home to several excellent branches of Wetherspoon's.

It

felt

like

a

secret

Nicole Flattery
Galway

When I was growing up, my mother worked. My father worked too but that was less shameful and awkward, more normal. I'd have several blank hours after school before my father returned so I was farmed out to other families. I lived in a small town, a village really, and day care was a suspicious, transatlantic idea. Day care—care all day. Already, at a young age, I was both disgusted and tempted by the idea of being totally looked after. And so it went, from the ages of eight to fifteen, I had two significant "other mothers." That was what I called them, disregarding my own mother or, perhaps, doing it deliberately to punish her. In the weekday afternoons, I stood on the fringes of these families, observed them and borrowed what I could from their lives. The first family I insinuated myself into was large, with five or six siblings, a huge father and a looming matriarch. It was like a family you would see on television, everyone accepting whatever was put on their plates, loving each other despite their flaws. They ate dinner together every evening at a long wooden table, cared little about homework, and played terrifying games of football, where it wasn't unusual to hear the crack of a bone amid the performative sliding. They had a girl the same age as I was and I styled myself on her, brushing out my hair and insisting, to everyone's disbelief, that I liked sports. I adopted her mannerisms too—her way of slumping over tables when she was bored, her rapid-fire dialogue. Everything I disliked about my own family (too

29

bookish, too absent) found its opposite in them. When I attempted to bring their loud customs back to my house—that short drive home felt like moving countries—my mother would be hurt, leave the room. Looking back, I don't know what the allure was. My own family was somehow both funnier and more serious. From that family, I stole discreet items: a pair of pyjamas, a couple of T-shirts. I remember once coming home with two tiny round tomatoes in my pockets, too terrified to tell my "other mother" I didn't like them and wanting, for some odd reason, to keep them as mementos. Then I became a teenager and moved to a more suitable family. It's rare to find a teenage girl with a fixed, definable personality. Most just plagiarise from whatever is available to them. The new family was perfect (high-achieving, blonde) in a shrill, histrionic way. It was the Ivanka Trump of families—if you pulled a single flawless string, all of it would shatter. I attempted to steal from them too, their haughty attitude (I failed), their excellent exam results (I generally failed). I remember my father asking me why I was studying with such insane devotion and, when I answered, "So I can be the best," he looked at me like I was an intruder in his home, a daughter-impersonator. I stole no goods from the perfect family. I admired them too much. And I would never have gotten away with it.

During that decade, the move in families, the change in temperament, I had one constant: I attended drama classes in a draughty town hall on Monday evenings. I was the star, but only in the sense that a room with nine cripplingly shy and speech-impediment-burdened children need a star. It was there I learned that if all art is "borrowing," then acting is basic theft. There's a famous anecdote about Marlon Brando watching James Dean enter a party and successfully predicting his every move.[1] Brando knew that Dean's personality, his dangerous allure, was stolen from his own and neutered to appeal to the masses. I did the same. I took elements of my "other mothers," years of being forced to observe women much older than I was, much more disappointed and strained, and I used them. These weren't very good performances. Do you think when Tennessee Williams wrote Blanche DuBois he imagined her being played by a seventeen-year-old with severe acne in the Midlands of Ireland?[2] I doubt it somehow. Still, this was my first taste of it, taking something from other people's lives and making it strange. I felt guilty about it. Years later, in college, where I studied film, a lecturer showed us how directors steal from the masters, referencing their heroes in their own films with similar shots, a near-identical cinematic language. He called it "homage"—and it didn't feel nasty or cheap. It felt like a secret.

Nicole[3]

---

1 This anecdote is from *Gods Like Us: On Movie Stardom and Modern Fame* by Ty Burr.

2 The writer is referring here to the 1947 Tennessee Williams play, *A Streetcar Named Desire*, which is set in New Orleans. The answer to the question here posed is almost certainly "no."

3 Nicole Flattery is a writer from the Midlands of Ireland. She studied theatre and film and has an M.Phil in creative writing from Trinity College, Dublin. Her

fiction and non-fiction has appeared in *The Stinging Fly*, *The Dublin Review*, *The Irish Times*, and on BBC Radio 4. She is working on a collection of short stories. When she was thirteen she had a pen pal from Berlin. Fearing she wasn't interesting enough, Nicole invented a lot of convoluted hobbies and interests, and had to sustain those lies for an unreasonable amount of time. It was, she reports, "very Adrian Mole."

we're
all
plagurists
of
each
othr

Andrew McMillan

Manchester

Dear Jon,

I think if you'd asked me to write this letter a few years ago, I might have objected more, but more recent years have seen me grow okay with talking about my professional relationship with my dad[1] (on a personal level, we're close as anything)—I was resistant, in the early days, to getting comments along the lines of "you're just here because of your dad" or "I bet I know how you got that job ..." I genuinely don't believe I got anything from nepotism but I know, in the same way a plagiarist is always caught out, that it would only get you so far; a magazine would never ask for another poem, a festival would never have you back again, if you didn't offer them something fresh & original & genuine.

Other industries seem fine with inheritance of interest, whether it's sons following fathers into industries, or trades, or folk music, or politics—only in writing does it seem that people have a real issue with it, and I think it's because we still pursue that old idea of the lone genius, anything that follows then must be plagiarism, be an imitation of what came before it—I don't think that's necessarily true. Yet of course I am like my dad, in mannerism, in voice (though not as much), in look (when our faces catch the light a certain way— all children are 50/50 copies of their parents/grandparents, children are plagiarised, young versions of their parents—my hairline, my height, my weight aren't my original ideas, I took them. My sisters are creative but not poets, you can't raise a poet or birth a poet, that part of the DNA is un-replicable.

One great tragedy/triumph of life is that we all end up copying our parents, their phrases, their shakes of the head, often their politics.[2]

Another thought, we're all plagiarists—of each other, of the world, of art. Even in the lexicon of you and your friends, how much of what you say is derived from a TV show (shouting the slogans from *RuPaul's Drag Race*[3] at each other), or maybe you now often say a phrase you learnt from a friend who learnt it from someone else— one day a sociologist or ethnographer will come in and find the "patient zero" of a particular phrase or inflection but until this you magpie from the world to build your own way of looking at it.

We're all plagiarists.

I am my father's son (I am self-plagiarising there, from one of my first published poems) but I am my own man too. So no, Jon, I don't mind talking about my relationship with my dad.

What's yours?[4]

Andrew[5]

---

1 Andrew McMillan's father is the well-known poet and broadcaster, Ian McMillan.

2 The writer may have had Oscar Wilde in mind at this point, writing in *The Importance of Being Earnest*: "All women become like their mothers. That is their tragedy. No man does, and that is his."

3 *RuPaul's Drag Race* is an American reality television series in which RuPaul and a panel of judges search for "America's next drag superstar."

4 This question is dealt with in a letter from the editor at the end of this volume.

5 Andrew McMillan is a poet from Barnsley, son of Ian McMillan, a poet from Barnsley. He has published three poetry pamphlets: *Every Salt Advance* (Red Squirrel Press, 2009), *The Moon Is A Supporting Player* (Red Squirrel Press, 2011), and *Protest Of The Physical* (Red Squirrel Press, 2013) as well as the award-winning full-length collection *Physical* (Jonathan Cape, 2015). *Physical* was the first poetry collection to win *The Guardian* First Book Award, and also won the Fenton Aldeburgh First Collection Prize, a Somerset Maugham Award (2016), an Eric Gregory Award (2016) and a Northern Writers' award (2014). Andrew lectures in creative writing at Liverpool John Moores University and lives in Manchester.

tables

forty

years

untouched

Chimene Suleyman
New York

To Whom This May Concern,

I don't know where home is.

I must tell you, as the child of immigrants, since I myself have migrated I found my understanding of it wrong. Perhaps, you think, you will possess more homes—only it has since occurred to me that you remain with even fewer. One cannot simply take a space and pass it off instinctively as our own. All that is innate becomes lost to you.

Nicosia, where my Turkish mother is from in Cyprus, stays divided through its belly.[1] Here, you may see what war looks like, frozen in time, an artefact of conflict.

No man's land is a peculiar name for a place, is it not?[2] How can you abandon streets and houses to the sky like this, and forbid all that was once human about it, it is incomprehensible.

There is a crudeness to the sandbags stacked one atop another, the barrels that have been pieced together to form a wall, the barbed wire that turns in on itself. It is not doing such a great job of concealing the houses behind them—in which case, when does a building become a house and not a home?

Help me find a way to describe the feeling one gets looking at the windows left open forty years. Did someone expect to go back to close them? I suppose they must have. What do tables forty years untouched look like? Cola bottles and picture frames?[3]

Four and a half miles at its widest point, eleven feet at its narrowest—it is paralysis. Neither Turkish nor Greek Cypriots allowed to walk in what were once their apartments, businesses, cafes or hotels. This is a stolen space, a place with no ownership—removed from reality and passed off as nothing.

My cousin, when we were younger, served his national service on one side of the border, looking into this abyss. On the other side, a young Greek Cypriot does the same.

You cannot ask two young men to look at homelessness like this, and expect them to see anything worth preserving. Certainly not when your line of sight shows that eventually everything is taken away—sooner given to nobody.

He tells me of one night of duty—that he and a soldier of the opposite side spent an evening rolling cigarettes across the narrow space to one another. Alongside this, magazines of naked girls. I think on this. They are no longer boys of a different language, a different religion—simply, they are boys.

And it is only when the slight space—which they have been told does not exist—is given purpose again, that they may recall intuitively what reclaiming home is, and build upon wherever this may be.

Chimene[4] X

1 Nicosia has been divided since 1964, when inter-communal violence, between Greek and Turkish Cypriots, erupted following decades of British colonial rule of the island. (Cyprus became independent in 1960). A buffer zone (see more details in the next footnote) was established in 1964; it was extended to its current size and became impassable in 1974 after the Turkish invasion of Cyprus, effectively dividing Nicosia (and Cyprus) into a northern (Turkish) and a southern (Greek) section.

2 Yes, no man's land *is* a peculiar name for a place. This demilitarised zone's official name is "The United Nations Buffer Zone in Cyprus," and it is under the control of the United Nations Peacekeeping Force in Cyprus (UNFICYP). It is also often referred to as: the UN Buffer Zone, the buffer zone, the cease-fire line, the Green Line, the dead zone, and the Attila Line. While uninhabited and abandoned in many places (as this letter describes), the buffer zone also includes farmlands and several villages where more than 10,000 people live and/or work. (One village, Pyla, is the only place on the island where Greek and Turkish Cypriots co-exist.) In other places, in the near absence of hunters and other human interference, the buffer zone has become a haven for flora and fauna.

3 The publishers have published a book on this very subject/question, with photographs of interiors of houses and buildings adjacent to the Green Line (*Nicosia in Dark and White* by Thodoris Tzalavras, Book Ex Machina, 2010), still-life pictures of a world frozen in time.

4 Chimene Suleyman is a poet and essayist. Her debut poetry collection, *Outside Looking On* (Influx Press, 2014), was one of *The Guardian*'s best books of the year in 2014. She has performed at the Royal Festival Hall, Book Slam, Literary Death Match, Bush Theatre, Latitude, Secret Garden Party, Standon Calling, Stratford Circus, Tongue Fu, and Outspoken. She has written on race and gender for *The Independent*, *Media Diversified*, and *The Quietus*. Chimene grew up in London and is currently based in New York.

"Thou Shalt Not Steal"

Darren Chetty
Hackney

Dear Editors,

Asked to write a letter about plagiarism, my first thought was to try something clever and original. I thought perhaps I could compose a letter made up entirely of sentences from other letters, and thus achieve some kind of unity between form and content. I skimmed numerous published letters, looking for sentences to repurpose, but soon realised that I'd set myself too difficult a challenge and that it would actually be much easier to use my own words.

I'm sure the irony is not lost on you. Contrary to the "make sure it's all your own work" mantra of the primary school classroom, careful copying is often harder than just doing your own thing. Rather than producing something that appears to be in no way related to anything previously created, it can be more difficult and rewarding to produce something that combines existing work into something new and coherent. It strikes me that this a fair summary of what I'm currently trying to do with my PhD thesis and, amongst other things, a decent summary of the genesis of hip-hop music.

Poet and educator Pie Corbett advocates teaching children how to write stories through the sequence *imitate, innovate, invent.*[1] In his film *Everything is a Remix*[2] Kirby Ferguson describes the basic element of creativity as *copy, combine, transform.* The tricolons might look and sound similar but by lowering the expectation of the final stage to "transform" from the grander "invent," Ferguson in fact may be presenting a more radical view of creativity in which the pre-existing source material always remains, however "original" the new work is.

DJ Kool Herc stood on the shoulders of giants in front of two turntables and a mixer, combining the breaks of funk, soul and rock records. In so doing, he transformed how people listened to the music, how they danced to it and, as his style became copied and transformed, how music was made. Legendary MC Grandmaster Caz said, "Hip-hop didn't invent anything, but hip-hop reinvented everything."[3] Maybe all creative acts are acts of reinvention? (Though perhaps it's worth noting that Caz also described the uncredited use of his lyrics on "Rapper's Delight" as "pure treason.")[4]

Charles Fairchild notes that "borrowing, appropriation, homage, derivation, allusion, re-composition, collage, pastiche and quotation" are "forms of musical creativity that have defined all kinds of music for centuries."[5] Clearly, this rich tradition wasn't enough to prevent Danger Mouse receiving a letter from Capitol over his mash-up of The Beatles' *White Album* and Jay Z's *The Black Album* that was his *The Grey Album*. Indeed, when rapper Biz Markie received a letter from Gilbert O'Sullivan's lawyers over his use of "Alone Again (Naturally)" it was, to many people, the beginning of the end of the golden age of hip-hop. Rappers found themselves being sued by musicians who, in many cases, had clearly borrowed and appropriated music themselves. The judge in the Biz Markie case saw this as clear-cut. "Thou Shalt Not Steal," he said, taking his words from a well-known publication (though it is not immediately clear whether he was referring to one of the many editions subject to copyright or one in the public domain).

Hip-hop's irreverence for copyright, its willingness to view everything as a potential source of material and to honour artists of the past ("Tell the truth, James Brown was old, till Eric and Ra came out with I got soul"),[6] are, I think, good reasons to take Mos Def's claim that "Hip-hop is a folk art" seriously. It is the conception of hip-hop that was at the heart of the Power to the Pupils project I ran in Hackney primary schools for five years and that informs the #HipHopEd UK seminars I put on with others. Acknowledging hip-hop in the primary classroom, I wanted to move away from the "rap writing as self-expression" model, where "self-expression" is taken to mean "write your own words; don't worry what anyone else has ever written."

Good rappers listen to rappers. Good writers read. Life experiences are crucial too, but you need to immerse yourself in the culture in order to learn the craft. You don't develop a sense of "self" in isolation from others, but rather through conversation with them. Expression is social. So the Power to the Pupils crew listened to hip-hop music, and to other styles of music that we could "sample" in some way. And at the same time we read widely. Raps were written that were clearly influenced by Karim, Tennyson, Seamus Heaney, Mary Shelley, Biggie Smalls, Johnny Cash, and Margaret Marie in year 5 to name but a few.

In opening up our range of influences to include an African diasporic art form that is itself open to diversity, we also exposed the boundaries that are often set in place through the curriculum and the stories we tell children. It was a series of letters to Charles Schulz that eventually persuaded him to introduce the first black character in *Peanuts*. Representation matters. As Chuck D notes, "Most of my heroes don't appear on no stamps."

In music, in writing, and in life there is perhaps nothing essentially "natural" about being alone (again). And I suspect Gilbert O'Sullivan must have known this—isn't that why in the first verse of his song he plans to throw himself off a tower?

Perhaps this assortment of quotes, thoughts, and anecdotes amounts to something worthwhile. It's a shame I couldn't pull off the fully plagiarised letter, but maybe someone else will make that a reality— I hope so.

With warm wishes,

Darren [7]

---

1 I see that Corbett has subsequently transformed this sequence into "imitation, innovation, independent application" which perhaps acknowledges my point here. See *Talk for Writing Across the Curriculum: How to teach non-fiction writing 5-12 years*, Pie Corbett and Julia Strong, McGraw Education, U.K. (2011).

2 *Everything is a Remix*, directed by Kirby Ferguson.

3 *Something from Nothing: The Art of Rap (2012)*, directed by ICE-T & Baybutt.

4 youtube.com/watch?v=wfh2cKl1hjs Video on YouTube: "Who is really responsible for 'Rappers Delight'? Grandmaster Caz explains why he's got beef with Big Bank Hank from Sugar Hill Gang."

5 *The Grey Album*, Charles Fairchild (2014), Bloomsbury, New York.

6 "Talkin all that Jazz" by Stetsasonic.

7 Darren Chetty is a teacher and a writer. Darren is a teaching fellow and doctoral candidate at University College London. He won an Award for Excellence in Philosophy for Children, presented by the International Council for Philosophical Inquiry with Children (ICPIC) for his article "The Elephant in the Room: Picturebooks, Philosophy for Children and Racism." He is a contributor to the essay collection, *The Good Immigrant* (Unbound, 2016), edited by Nikesh Shukla.

they don't know why
he's worried about
copyright

16th June 2016

Dear Readers,

The other day I was in Newhaven on the south coast. The town is a desperate place of boarded-up shops. Among the few that cling on is *{redacted}*, a second-hand bookshop owned by a posh older bloke with a red face, who always seems half-cut. He sits outside, reading *The Times,* and smiles mildly when you go in. His stock, which seems to have come from various house clearances many years ago, is piled higgledy-piggledy with no attempt at order. It smells of damp. Classic FM plays in the background.

As I now have a family, albeit a small one, I picked up a cookery book entitled *Family Meals*, published in 1977 by Marks & Spencer, part of the St Michael Cookery Library. I wondered why and when M&S got rid of that St Michael brand and as I flicked through garish pictures of chicken pies and lasagnas, I found tucked between pages 72 and 73 (which had recipes for vanilla ice cream and Melba sauce, with ingredients in imperial measures) a letter from Jason to Kim, typed on a page torn from a hole-punched notebook on 5th June 1982. Jason of 50, *{redacted}* Avenue, Surbiton, Surrey (no insistence on postcodes in those days). Jason of the flamboyant signature and the four kisses. Jason who has sent Kim at least one poem and written many more. Jason who thinks of Kim every day in bad French.

In my mind, Kim looks like Kim Wilde. She is beautiful and kind, but slightly aloof from the lovelorn Jason. I sense he is lovelorn. It is Kim who he pines for as he sits at home on a Saturday night, typing out his poems and waiting for his mysterious Monday operation which will enable him to work again and "feel a lot better."

Kim is more alluring than the "young lady" who keeps calling him up and "getting too close." Kim, though, has written a recipe for a pavlova on the back of Jason's letter and casually used it as a bookmark. She thought about making vanilla ice cream for her first ever dinner party, but it's too much bother; she'll buy a striped block of Neapolitan from the Spar and serve it in slices with her pavlova. She's off to France in August. She will have a good time there, as Jason predicts, a Gauloise between her red lips, sunglasses perched on her bleached blonde hair. She won't think about Jason much and when she does she'll feel guilty pity. She and Nikki, their mutual friend, worry about him. They wish he'd find a girlfriend, they hope he'll get a proper job after his operation and stop fantasizing about being a poet and songwriter. His poems have never been published and no one famous has ever sung his songs so they don't know why he's worried about copyright.

They like him though. He's sweet and open, too open—almost naïve. They've known him since school. They used to hang out at lunchtime on the playing field, reading *Smash Hits* and then *NME* when they got older and were trying to be cool. He got on better with girls than boys. He wasn't into football and fighting and the other boys called him a "poofter." In fact, Nikki and Kim wonder if Jason is actually gay but can't admit it to himself. It is becoming easier to be gay these days—look at Boy George. But Boy George

5▓, ▓▓▓▓▓▓ Avenue,
SURBITON,
Surrey.

5th June 1982

Dear KIm,

Thank you for your letter, which I received
this morning. I am glad you liked the poem. By the time you received
this letter I will have had that operation I have been waiting for.
I go into hospital tomorrow (sunday), and they operate on Monday. I
cannot wait I have been waiting for months!, also when it is over and
done with I will be able to start work again which will make me feel
a lot better.

I have typed out a lot of my poems' and lyrics'
so I can get them copyrighted, I have so many which I have written over
the years I do not know where to start. I do not know which are worth
having copyrighted or not, or any of them are worth copyrighting.
Not alot has happened this way, having a bit of a problem with a young
lady I know. She keeps' calling me up and getting too close, I am just
not interested and I find it difficult to tell her or anyone as a matter
of fact, to back of, oh well I will think of something I always do.

Nikki told me you were going to France about
August time, but I was not too sure about the exact dates, I hope you
have a good time (which I know you will) but no doubt I will hear or
see you before then, I hope. Any way, I must love you and leave you
and I will hear from you soon, and I will call you soon. Look after
yourself and give my love to Nikki if you hear from her.

Love you as always

[signature]

P.S Je pense á' toi toujours ▓▓▓ ma chér.

xxxx

51

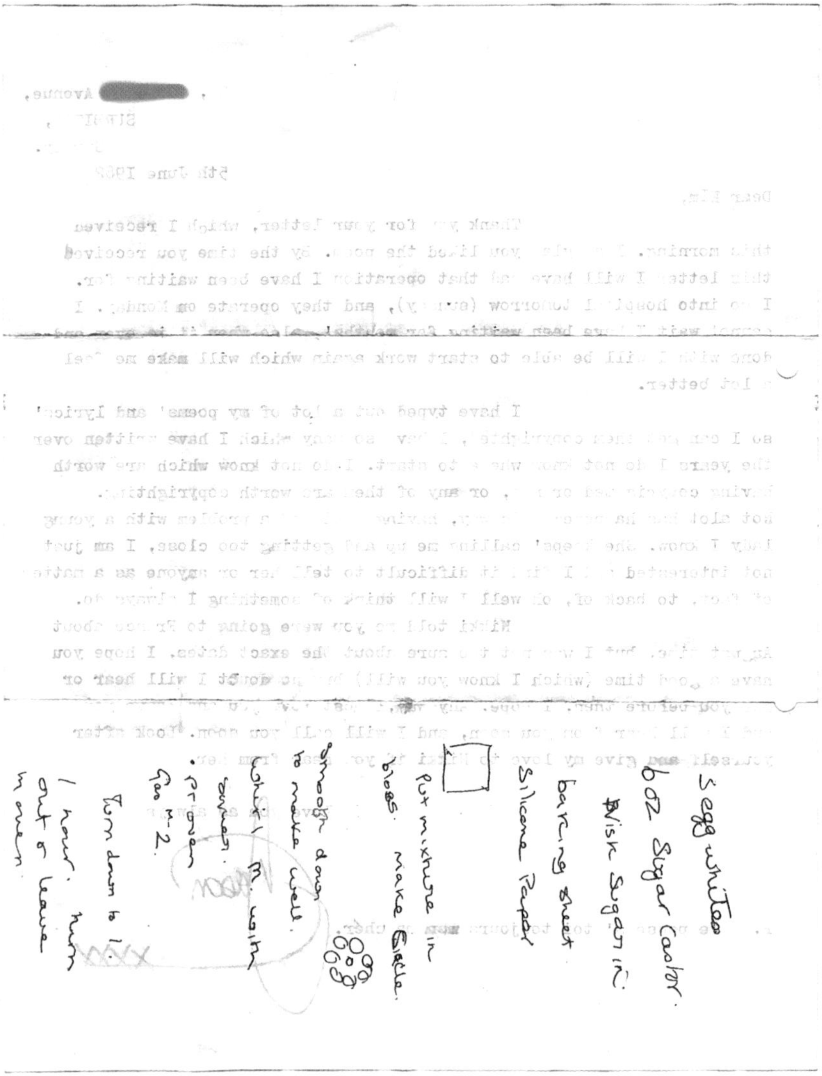
5 egg whites
6 OZ Sugar Castor.
Wisk Sugar in.
baking sheet.
Silicone Paper
Put mixture in
blobs. make Circle.
Smooth down
to make well.
Whisk M. with
cream.
. Pr oven
Gas M 2.
Turn down to 1.
1 hour. turn
out or leave
in oven.

doesn't live in Surbiton with his mum. Maybe one day Jason will come out, leave Surbiton for Brighton where Kim now lives and they'll go clubbing. That's if Kim's husband, who she hasn't yet met in 1982, allows her a night off from the kids and cooking Family Meals from the old recipe book her mum lent her when she went off to art college.

Where are they now, Kim, Nikki and Jason? I reckon they're in their early–to–mid 50s, judging by their names. They were in their late teens to early twenties then, still finding themselves, still with time to write letters and poems and have intense friendships. Does Nikki still write her name with circles above the i's, or hearts when she's feeling extra cheeky? Has Kim split up from her boring husband who never really understood anything about her, including why she would be friends with someone like Jason? Did she chuck out *Family Meals* when the family home broke up? And, Jason, did he ever get his poems published? Does he still think about Kim *toujours*? Does he still have her old letters? Does he ever re-read them? And if he does, does he feel as much nostalgia for the '80s, the era of my childhood, as I do, reading his letter thirty-four years after he wrote it?

À bientôt,

Rowena [1] x

---

1 Rowena Macdonald was born on the Isle of Wight, grew up in the West Midlands, and now lives in East London. Her debut collection of short stories, *Smoked Meat* (Flambard Press, 2011), was short-listed for the 2012 Edge Hill Prize. Her debut novel, *The Threat Level Remains Severe*, was published in July 2017 by Aardvark Bureau, an imprint of Gallic Books. Rowena lives in London, and works in the House of Commons.

no-one

leaves

this

town

dehydrated

Sarah Dale
Évian-les-Bains, France

8th September 2016

A letter to anyone who has suffered from a urinary tract infection:

Riding a hired bike with a monumentally unforgiving saddle for 25 miles, whilst menopausal, turns out to be something of a health risk. From that evening onwards, acute cystitis suddenly sets in. I've occasionally suffered before (is there a woman who hasn't?) but this is particularly intense. It is miserable and makes me wonder how many people are battling on silently around us. I drink enough water to nearly drown myself (but not my sorrows, which continue), buy cranberry extract from La Pharmacie, cry a little, sleep a lot, don't venture out. On the third day, common sense (and high fever) prevail and I visit the doctor. A single sachet of miracle powder dissolved in water and I'm on the mend. (We'll miss antibiotics when they no longer work.)

We are en vacances, in the French Alps, and we arrive in Évian, on the shores of Lake Geneva. I feel weakened, ready to surrender to the resort's reputation for health promotion and convalescence. I'm in the right place to recover from my "maladie," as it's described on the insurance form provided by the doctor. Maladie feels like the correct term.

In 1789, I discover, Count Jean-Charles de Laizer came here to take the waters for his kidney stones. (And—quel bonus—escape the revolution. Back then, this area wasn't in France.) After "repeated drinking" his health improved and the Evian industry was born (7 million bottles a day are now produced). I attach a picture which shows him ~~avoiding the guillotine~~ curing his urinary problems. I drink another glass-full, and wonder whether the women with him are silently in "maladie" sans antibiotics.

I guess no-one leaves this town dehydrated. Urine colour "paint" charts are freely available,[1] and water pours, day and night, from the wall at Source Cachet. There is no excuse. I write on appropriately coloured paper (is it coincidence that goods are served in bags of this hue?)—check your urine colour now!

UTI sufferers know all this. For some unlucky souls, no amount of water or avoiding nearly everything enjoyable (cycling, wine, coffee, sugar, sex …) stops infection. I have no answers, but send sympathy and hugs from the gentille, beautiful, bladder-aware, town of Évian-les-Bains,

Sarah[2] x

1 The writer has included one of these colour charts, which asks "Êtes-vous suffisamment hydratés?" (Are you getting enough hydration?) The chart offers a range of colours, from the tepid yellow "Vous avez assez bu" (you have drunk enough), down to the alarmingly brown "Vous ne buvez vraiment pas assez" (you appear not to have drunk any water for days and your bladder is ruined, get thee to a physician immediately).

2 Sarah Dale is an occupational psychologist with an interest in writing. She is based in Nottingham, where she runs her own business. She has published *Keeping Your Spirits Up* (Creating Focus, 2011) and *Bolder and Wiser* (Creating Focus, 2014).

I'm not sure

who

this is

addressed to

Jonathan Ellis [1]
Sheffield

1/

A letter:

On 25 May my Dad died suddenly in his sleep. I've written that sentence so many times in the last few months that I almost believe it to be true.

2/

I don't really know if it was sudden or in his sleep. I don't even know if it was 25 May. Perhaps it was the day before. Around midnight

3/

For the last two weeks of his life Dad didn't eat or drink. He had what most people euphemistically call a "water infection." It hurt when he went to pee.

4/

Dad's solution to this problem was to stop drinking. He gave up liquid in stages. First tea. Then orange juice. Then milk.

5/

He never gave up water because he never drank water.

6/

"Dad, you can't stop drinking," I said. "You're going to die."

Not believing me, or perhaps believing me, the last drink he gave up was Lucozade.

"Everything else tastes of metal."

7/

The water infection didn't kill him. The death certificate said it was a secondary cause.

8/

On arriving at the house I found his last letter. It was written to himself as much as anybody else. A rectangular yellow Post-It note, reminding himself to give Mum her insulin and to shave. He also wrote the PIN of his debit card in the top right-hand corner. He couldn't seem to remember numbers the last few months.

9/

He gave Mum insulin twice a day. Remembering it was one of the last things he remembered to do.

10/

I don't know if he remembered to shave. I forgot to ask my brother.

11/

The PIN worked for a week until the bank received the letter he was dead.

12/

They wrote me a letter to apologise. "You may still continue to receive letters addressed to your father."

13/

Yes. They keep arriving.

14/

Subscriptions to *Time* magazine. *National Geographic.* The Open University.

15/

Other banks.

16/

Debt companies.

17/

The occasional postcard.

18/

Circulars. Reminders.

19/

I probably need to redirect this post when the family house is sold.[2]

20/

"Don't tell your brother I'm not eating," were I think his final words.

21/

Or 6206 on the Post-It note.

22/

They probably mean something I'll never know.

23/

If you know, can you tell me?

24/

I'm not sure who this is addressed to but it's by me.

25/

Jonathan Ellis

26/

P.S. I bought this paper in a Japanese stationary shop in Montreal[3] on my honeymoon eight years ago. This is the first time I've used it.

27/

P.P.S. My Dad's Post-It notes were not half as beautiful. But I've kept them all. For safe keeping. Even the last one.

---

1 Jonathan Ellis teaches at the University of Sheffield. His edited book, *Letter Writing Among Poets: From William Wordsworth to Elizabeth Bishop*, was published in 2016.

2 According to the author: "The house, which my parents lived in since 1971, was sold on 9 October. The last thing I took from the house was a handful of cooking apples from a neighbour's tree that overhangs the back garden; I left some for the new owners. The post has been re-directed."

3 On recollection, the author wonders whether he in fact bought this paper in Japan in 2004 on a trip to interview the Japanese novelist, Haruki Murakami. Wherever he bought it, the paper was definitely made in Japan.

Five Pieces of 250 Words:
A Bibliography

On Big Bill Broonzy's *Trouble in Mind* album there are nineteen songs, of which twelve were recorded around March 1957 at the Dancing Slipper club on Central Avenue in West Bridgford at a concert organised by a one-armed jazz promoter whose nickname was Lefty.

Although I didn't know the titles of any of his albums, I'd heard a couple of tapes by Big Bill Broonzy, and when I filled in a *wants* card at Good Vibrations on Mansfield Road I just listed the names of all the songs of his that I had come across.

The book *Big Bill Blues* features an account of how a black woman, who'd imagined it would be easier to find work in Chicago than in the South, queues all day in an employment office only for her number never to get called, to which Broonzy comments, "It's the same soup, but it's just served in a different way."

The footage in which Big Bill Broonzy sits in the sun on the porch of a wooden house and strums "Stump Blues" and "Hey, Hey" was made the day before he underwent his operation for throat cancer, in July 1957, and was shot by Pete Seeger on a 16mm Auricon camera.

As I write this the sky is already a deep smudgy blue and though the days are still warm and it'll be weeks before we even begin thinking about college, something of the hush of autumn is nudging its way into my understanding of things.

While it is broadly understood that Pete Seeger's response to Bob Dylan's use of an electric guitar and an amplified backing band at the 1965 Newport Folk Festival was to take an axe to the electrical cables, it has been suggested[2] that this is a misunderstanding which grew out of a comment made onstage by the festival announcer during the moments of cheering and booing following the three-song set of electric blues.

At least some of the people in the audience were calling for Dylan to return to the stage with an acoustic guitar, and while in the announcer's use of the phrase "he's gonna get his axe," "he" has usually been taken to refer to Seeger and "axe" has usually been understood in literal terms, the possibility that the pronoun was in fact being used to refer to Dylan and "axe" was being used as hipster slang for guitar puts things into a different perspective.

The fact that earlier that July day Pete Seeger had given a performance of a traditional work song in which he had kept time by chopping wood with an authentic lumberjack's axe may be an element in the way this matter has been perceived.

My copy of the live album of Pete Seeger's 1963 concert at Carnegie Hall was among the many Pete Seeger records in the second-hand racks at Good Vibrations.

As I write this there are crows on the greenhouse roof and the snow on the windowsills is already beginning to thaw.

Of the ten songs on Bob Dylan's *Modern Times* album, four use the structure of the twelve-bar blues.

The sixteen verses of "The Levee's Gonna Break" are bunched into fours, with a guitar solo after each bunch. The repetition of the title phrase is perhaps a defining element of the song's structure. In two of the verses the phrase "some of these people" is sung in the concluding line; in two of the others the phrase "some people" is used.

In "Someday Baby" the first two lines of each verse comprise a rhyme. The unrhymed third line is identical in all nine verses.

The words of "Thunder on the Mountain" fit into quatrains with an aabb rhyme scheme. One couplet is sung over the first four bars and the second is stretched across the next eight. The twelve verses of the song are bunched into threes, and each bunch is rounded off with a guitar break. The title phrase is sung in the first line of the first verse in each bunch.

"The Levee's Gonna Break" and "Rollin' and Tumblin'" are both blues of the kind in which the second line is a restatement of the first.

At the time of the record's release *The Observer* published an interview Bob Dylan gave to Jonathan Lethem.

I downloaded the record track-by-track with LimeWire, though when my misgivings got the better of me I bought it for £5 from Fopp.

As I write this there are blackbirds gathering twigs in my yard.

In its examination of what the idea of creativity might involve, Jonathan Lethem's essay "The Ecstasy of Influence" discusses how the description Muddy Waters gives of the way he wrote his song "Country Blues" includes a number of possibly contradictory accounts, including being taught it by another guitar player, it coming from the cotton field, and, as he was fixing a puncture and feeling blue about a girl, the song falling into his mind.

While the first Jonathan Lethem book I read was *The Fortress of Solitude*, which at the time I bought it had been published four years, and the second was *Motherless Brooklyn*, which had been published eight years, the first I was able to respond to as something entirely new—I remember reading a review in *The Guardian* and seeing copies of it piled on the *recent releases* table in the Arndale Centre branch of Waterstone's—was *You Don't Love Me Yet*, which came out in 2007.

As I write this it feels like nothing can disturb the stuffy summery heat, and the imprecision that's getting into everything is meaning the bed linen is feeling scratchy and the radio is playing louder and the flies in the kitchen have it in mind that by circulating beneath the strip lights in a loosely triangular formation they'll somehow come to terms with the principles on which things interact, and then the drizzle will drag in through the city again and our voices will become unresonant and tuneless and raspy.

In the footage of his 1977 concert at the Molde Jazz Festival, the audience doesn't applaud the piano solo in "Prison Bound Blues" until Muddy Waters explicitly prompts them to. The volume switches on Muddy Waters's Telecaster were the *chickenhead* switches he had removed from his amplifier.

Unless I play it at maximum volume, the album of Big Bill Broonzy songs recorded by Muddy Waters in 1960, which I downloaded from iTunes, can be particularly difficult to listen to.

Muddy Waters began using an electric guitar and playing with an amplified backing band when he moved to Chicago from Mississippi in 1943.

The performance that a number of American blues singers gave in the rain at Wilbraham Road station was broadcast by Granada TV in 1964. There's an extended passage in the footage of Muddy Waters's 1960 Newport Jazz Festival performance which features close-ups of the feet of audience members twitching in time to the music. When Fender produced its Artist Series Muddy Waters Telecaster, it came with the amplifier switches already fitted.

I bought the DVD of the performances at the jazz festivals at Newport, Copenhagen, and Molde from the Rough Trade shop in Portobello Road. During the encore at the Newport concert Muddy Waters dances ballroom-style with his harmonica player.

As I write this there's a dripping tap keeping time with the recording of "You're Gonna Miss Me (When I'm Dead and Gone)" and the breeze from the kitchen window is ruffling the pencil sharpenings piled on my desk.

BIBLIOGRAPHY[3]

[4]Big Bill Broonzy, *Trouble in Mind*, LP, Spotlite SPJ900 (1957).

Big Bill Broonzy with Yannick Bruynoghe, *Big Bill Blues*, (New York, Da Capo, 1992).

No explanation is given for the jump in point size between the introduction and forewords, and the main body of the text.

Pete, Toshi and Dan Seeger, *A Musical Journey*, DVD, Vestapol 13042 DVD (1957-64).

Bob Dylan, *The Other Side of the Mirror*, DVD, Columbia 88697144669 (1963-65).

Elijah Wald, *Dylan Goes Electric!: Newport, Seeger, Dylan, and the Night that Split the Sixties*, (New York, Dey Street Books, 2015).

If it is possible for the facts to fit a theory too snugly, Wald's discussion of the use of the term "axe" may be a good example.

Pete Seeger, *We Shall Overcome*, LP, CBS BPG62209 (1963).

Bob Dylan, *Modern Times*, CD, Columbia 82876876062 (2006).

Jonathan Lethem, *The Ecstasy of Influence*, (London, Jonathan Cape, 2012).

Jonathan Lethem, *The Fortress of Solitude*, (London, Faber, 2005).

Jonathan Lethem, *Motherless Brooklyn*, (London, Faber, 2004).

Patrick Ness, "Lost in La-La Land," *The Guardian*, 14 July 2007.

Jonathan Lethem, *You Don't Love Me Yet*, (London, Faber, 2007).

Muddy Waters, *Classic Concerts*, DVD, Universal 0602498741290 (1960-77).

Muddy Waters, *Muddy Waters Sings "Big Bill"*, MP3 download, Geffen (1960).

The amplified band's interpretations of Broonzy's tunes might be regarded as the stencil[5] for the albums of Robert Johnson material recorded by Eric Clapton and Peter Green.

Muddy Waters and others, *The American Folk-Blues Festival*, DVD, Hip-O Records 0602517205888 (1963-66).

Muddy Waters, *The Complete Plantation Recordings*, CD, MCA CHD9344 (1941-42).

---

1 "Five Pieces of 250 Words: A Bibliography." While the content of these five pieces creates its own circular—or, perhaps more accurately, pentagonal—poetic form, the extent to which much of Matthew Welton's writing is characterised by the preponderance of six-word lines, six-line stanzas, six-stanza poems, and so on, gave "Five pieces, each of 250 words" something of an incongruity. With the addition of a sixth piece that problem disappears. It is for this reason that the bibliography is included.

2 Although these five pieces were composed with the conceptual imperative that the only people whose names may be included in each are the individual on whom that piece centres and the individual on whom the subsequent piece will centre, the decision to use the passive "it has been suggested" and avoid making a proper attribution naming the writer whose suggestion it is creates the ethical problem of using un-cited sources. It is for this reason that the bibliography is included.

3 Since 2010 Matthew Welton has felt a need to express support for the Footnote Moratorium Cessation Treaty (Proposed) though until now he had been unable to come up with the appropriate vehicle through which to do that. It is for this reason that the bibliography is included.

4 In spite of his inordinate fondness for the word "stencil," the difficulty Matthew Welton encountered in attempting to shoehorn it into any of the original five pieces caused him to seek an ulterior method by which it might be admitted. It is for this reason that the bibliography is included.

5 Matthew Welton was born in Nottingham in 1969. Matthew received the Jerwood Aldeburgh First Collection Prize for *The Book of Matthew* (Carcanet, 2003). His second collection was *We needed coffee but we'd got ourselves convinced that the later we left it the better it would taste, and, as the country grew flatter and the roads became quiet and dusk began to colour the sky, you could guess from the way we returned the radio and unfolded the map or commented on the view that the tang of determination had overtaken our thoughts, and when, fidgety and untalkative but almost home, we drew up outside the all-night restaurant, it felt like we might just stay in the car, listening to the engine and the gentle sound of the wind* (Carcanet, 2009). His third collection, *The Number Poems*, was also published by Carcanet in September 2016. Matthew collaborates regularly with the composer Larry Goves, with whom he was awarded a Jerwood Opera Writing Fellowship in 2008. Matthew is an assistant professor in creative writing at the University of Nottingham.

Say hi to your dad from me

Jon McGregor
Nottingham

Dear Andrew,

Thanks for your letter,[1] and sorry it's taken me a while to get back to you. I wasn't imagining writing back to you—we get quite a lot of letters here at *The Letters Page*, and I'm not generally in the habit of writing replies, even when the letter delights my editorial soul and I decide to publish it—but you asked me a direct question and I feel like it could do with an answer.

"I don't mind talking about my relationship with my dad," you said; "what's yours?"

Well. It's funny you should ask.

My dad was a vicar, and apart from a brief lapse at around the age of five I never wanted to follow in his footsteps. But it's been dawning on me lately how much I learnt from him all the same, and how much my work has in common with his. I work from home, as he did, at all sorts of unpredictable hours. (Although, to be fair, no-one ever calls me late at night wanting to arrange a funeral, or knocks at the door asking for sandwiches.) My work revolves around words; his, The Word.[2] The walls of my home are lined with books, which I turn to when I get stuck or lost in what I'm doing, and this is a habit I've surely inherited from him. We have both ended up in a role that asks us to stand up in front of people and talk, when that's the last thing either of us would voluntarily do – and yet we secretly both quite enjoy it.

Dammit, I even look like him. I mean, obviously I've always looked like him a bit, sharing genes as we do, but I saw a new photo of myself recently and it's starting to look uncanny. And then I recently recorded myself reading aloud, working on getting the hang of doing so when my next novel comes out, and was shocked to hear that I sounded almost exactly like my dad, in church, reading the liturgy. (I was doing "poet voice," as it turns out. And the conversation about influence and the contagion of "poet voice" is one we can save for another day.)

I guess the point I'm making is that whether we follow in their footsteps or not, we can never really escape the influence of our parents. We do, as you said, plagiarise them to some extent. In behaviour, in voice, in gesture. There's a particular way I have of resting my chin in my hand—forefinger almost touching my ear, my other fingers making a moustache, so that my chin is only in fact resting on my thumb—which when I catch myself doing it reminds me vividly of my father.

And it's those tiny things that make me miss him the most. He died nearly two years ago. (I've written about this before, in an editor's note in Issue 6 of *The Letters Page*, but hey, sometimes you have to talk about these things more than once.) Sometimes it feels like I miss him more now than I did in those first few weeks or months. It turns out that the human brain—or this human brain, at least—takes quite a while to comprehend what "gone" really means. Permanent doesn't feel permanent right away. I thought that after the passing of a year, and all the obvious first milestones, the hard part would be done. But in fact there are plenty of milestones that aren't annual at all, but just crop up from time to time in a life and make you think, oh, hey, I can't wait to tell Dad about this.

I've just taught a class on Lydia Davis. It's the same class I taught last year. We looked at a story called "Grammar Questions,"[3] which features a narrator worrying about the correct tenses to use to refer to her dying father.

"If someone asks me, 'Where does he live?' can I say, 'He lives in Vernon Hall'? Or should I say, 'He is dying in Vernon Hall'?"

The story is brilliantly dry and pedantic, and all the more moving for it, and is an almost perfect description of my state of mind during the three absurdly short weeks when my father moved from illness to diagnosis and death. How do you describe those moments, day by day, when you can't be sure until after the fact what the chronology actually is? But here's the point; when I read the story to the class last year, I was fine. This year, I had to cut it short. The way this works is going to be unpredictable, it turns out.

So, to answer your question: the relationship I had with my father was a lovely one, straightforward and loving and full of humour. The relationship I have with my father now is a relationship to those memories, and to the fact of his death. I guess you could say it has its ups and downs.

Thanks for your letter, Andrew. Say hi to your dad from me.

Regards,

Jon

1 See earlier in this volume.

2 The writer is here using a traditional theological term to refer to the Bible, and not referring to the seminal Channel 4 youth-oriented television programme of the 1990s.

3 *The Collected Stories of Lydia Davis*, Hamish Hamilton, 2009.

4 Jon McGregor is the author of four novels and a story collection. He is the winner of the IMPAC Dublin Literature Prize, Betty Trask Prize, and Somerset Maugham Award, and has twice been longlisted for the Man Booker Prize. He is a professor of creative writing at the University of Nottingham, where he founded and edits *The Letters Page*. His latest novel, *Reservoir 13*, was published by 4th Estate earlier this year.